Banana tree

2

3

Water lily

Hop like a frog.

Roar like a tiger.

1

Hiss like a snake.

Squawk like a parrot.

4

Howl like a howler monkey.

Bare your teeth like a piranha.

8

Stay very still like a sloth.

5

Orchid

Wave your arm like an elephant's trunk.

7

6

Vines

USBORNE

FORTUNE TELLERS
TO FOLD

Written by Lucy Bowman

Illustrated by Anne Passchier, Essi Kimpimaki and Alex Westgate

Designed by Jodie Smith, Melissa Gandhi and Amy Manning

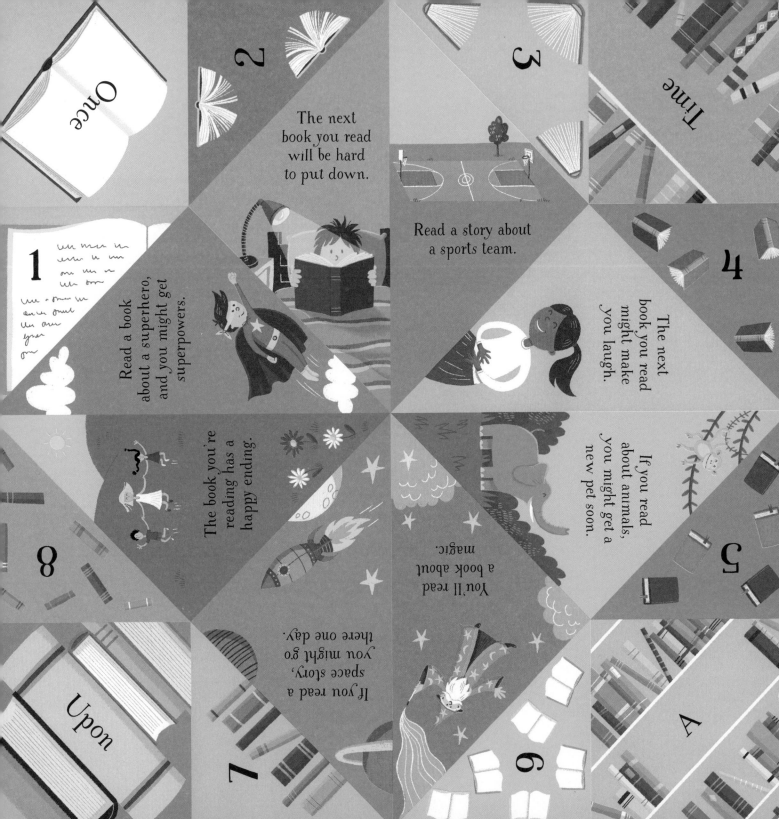

Once

2

3

Time

1

The next
book you read
will be hard
to put down.

Read a story about
a sports team.

4

Read a book
about a superhero,
and you might get
superpowers.

The next
book you read
might make
you laugh.

The book you're
reading has a
happy ending.

If you read
about animals,
you might get a
new pet soon.

8

You'll read
a book about
magic.

5

Upon

If you read a
space story,
you might go
there one day.

6

A

7

Ghost

2

There's a skeleton behind your door.

3

Skeleton

1

Don't drink a magic potion.

You'll enjoy eyeballs for dinner.

4

Your next meal will be worm pie.

There's a monster under your bed.

Your breakfast might be a moss smoothie —yum!

Watch out! There's a ghost in your mirror.

Look out! Flying witch overhead.

8

Mummy

7

6

5

Monster

Dragon

Princess

2

3

4

Don't worry — a knight will rescue you!

Beware of an old woman bearing a gift.

1

Kiss a frog and it could turn into someone else...

If you hear a mermaid singing — don't listen.

If you find a beanstalk, you should climb it.

A wizard will put a spell on you!

A fairy godmother will grant you three wishes.

8

Someone you know is a wolf in disguise.

5

Castle

Wicked witch

7

6

Basketball

2

3

Tennis

1

The more times you bounce a ball, the more luck you'll have.

Throw and catch a ball, and you'll get a surprise.

Next time you play mini golf, you'll get a hole in one.

If you enter a swimming race, you might win.

4

If you play basketball, you might make three shots.

Each time you kick a ball in the air, a wish will come true.

8

Score a goal and you'll be player of the match.

Play 'catch' with a friend and you'll hear good news.

5

Soccer

7

6

Golf

Winter

Snow

2

3

A winter
nap will bring
you good dreams.

One day you'll
learn to ice skate.

1

4

Next time it
snows, you'll have
an adventure.

Stay home
tonight with
a good book.

Don't forget to
wrap up warm
this winter.

If you
make a snow
angel, you'll
have good luck.

8

5

If you see tracks
in the snow, guess
what made them.

You'll sleep
soundly in
your warm
bed tonight.

Ice

7

6

Cold

Heart

2

3

Lovebirds

You have a
secret admirer.

Someone likes you,
but you don't feel
the same.

1

4

The person
you like likes
you back.

You'll get a
Valentine's gift.

You'll meet
someone
special soon.

You'll send a
Valentine's card
– but to whom?

You'll get a
mysterious
Valentine's card.

8

5

You have a
secret crush
on someone.

Cupid

7

6

Rose

What's

Name?

Your

Pirate

1
2
3
4
5
6
7
8

You're Scallywag Scourge, matey.

You're known as Jumpy Jones.

Your pirate name is Bearded Beast.

Your nickname is Treasure Hunter.

Peg Leg is a good name for you.

They call you Grog Breath.

Ahoy there, Crazy Crab!

Your nickname is Scurvy Eyes.

1

2

3

4

A creature with a shell might be a good pet for you.

You might choose a pet that can swim.

If you play with a cat, it might be your friend.

Your next pet could be covered in fur.

You might get a pet with a long tail.

A spider might be a good pet for you.

A pet that hops could bring good fortune.

Your next pet might have wings.

5

6

8

7

Clown

2

Spin a hoop around your waist for 30 seconds.

Do a drum roll.

3

Ringmaster

1

Learn to juggle with two balls.

Tell jokes like a clown.

4

Pretend to walk along a tightrope.

Flex your muscles like a strong man.

Try out some acrobatics.

Pretend to be a ringmaster.

5

8

Circus tent

7

6

Acrobat

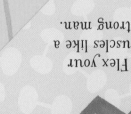

Eggs

2

3

Easter Bunny

1

You might find some Easter eggs on a hunt.

Cheep like a chick.

4

If you break an egg at Easter, it means good luck.

The Easter Bunny could bring you lots of eggs.

If you see bright flowers, it may mean it's spring.

If you get a chocolate bunny, you might see a real bunny soon.

8

Hop like a bunny.

5

Spring

If you decorate some eggs, give them to your friends.

7

6

Chick

Shooting star

2

3

Horseshoe

If you break a mirror, you may have seven years bad luck.

You could find a pot of gold.

1

Hang a red lantern and your luck could change.

4

If you step on a crack, you may have bad luck.

You might be unlucky if you open an umbrella indoors.

8

Do a good deed and you may have good fortune.

If you see a rainbow, it means you'll be lucky.

5

Four-leaf clover

7

Try not to walk under a ladder — you could have bad luck.

6

Black cat

Cake

2

3

Present

1

The birthday cake might be chocolate.

If you win a party game, it means you're lucky.

4

You might see an amazing magic trick.

You might be invited to a pirate party soon.

If you blow out candles in one try, you'll get an extra wish.

8

You might be given a bear for your birthday.

You could get an art set as a gift.

The next party you go to might be a sleepover.

5

Party

7

6

Balloon

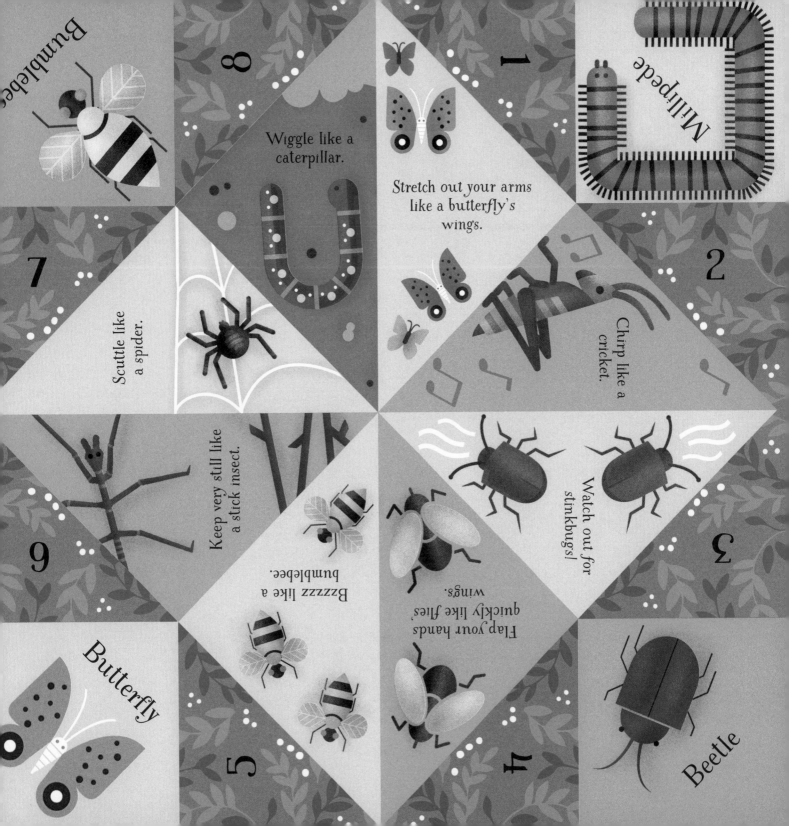

What

Eat?

Should

1

2

3

4

5

6

7

8

You'll try some seafood.

You'll cook spaghetti.

You'll eat hot soup.

You'll eat a juicy burger.

You'll make your own burrito.

You'll nibble on kebabs.

You'll munch on a healthy salad.

You'll eat delicious fried dumplings.

What

Do?

Will

You

1

2

3

4

5

6

7

8

Fly a kite.

Make a big splash.

Spot lots of seashells.

Write a message in the sand.

Make a sundial.

Build a sandcastle.

Make a mermaid tail out of sand.

Search for sea creatures.

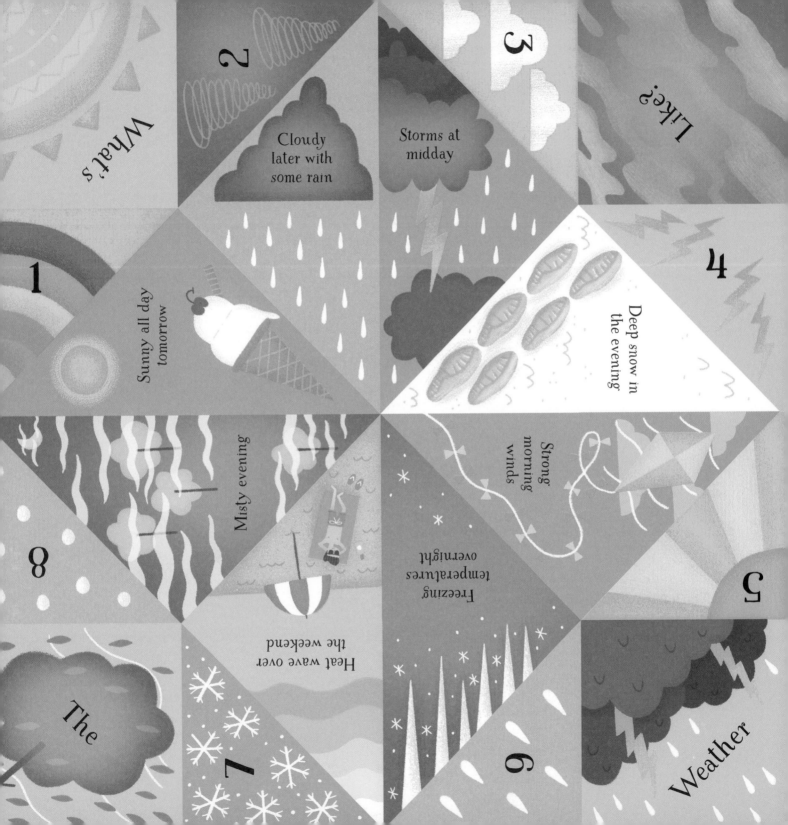

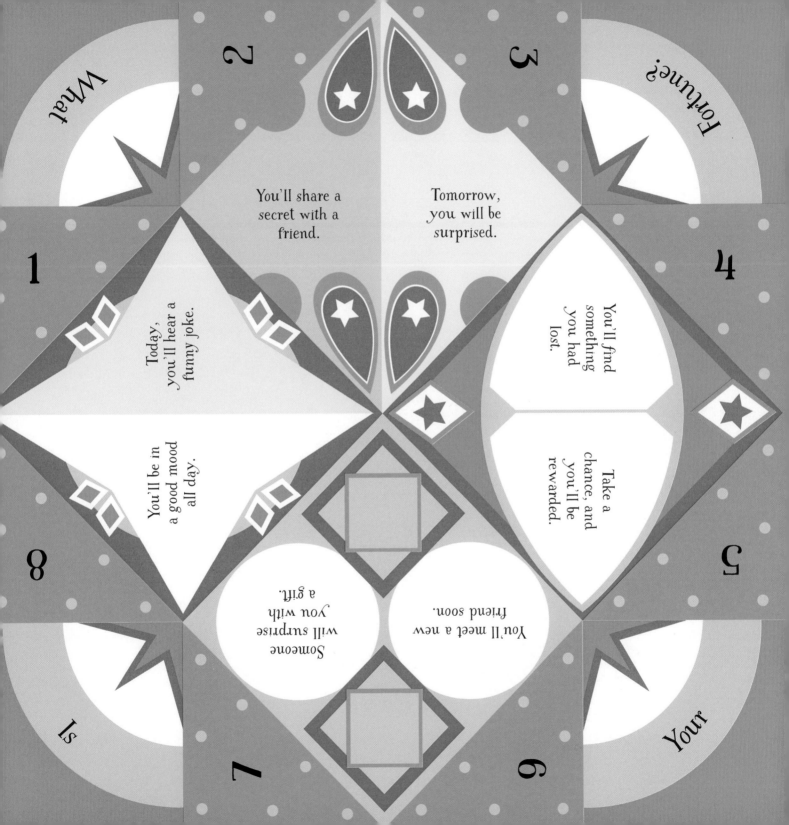

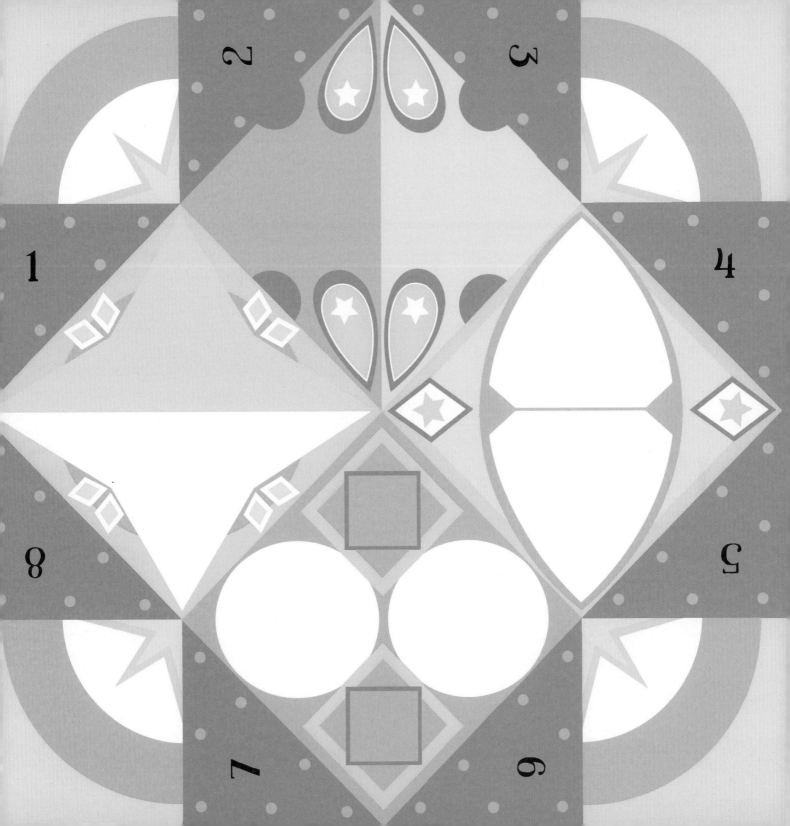

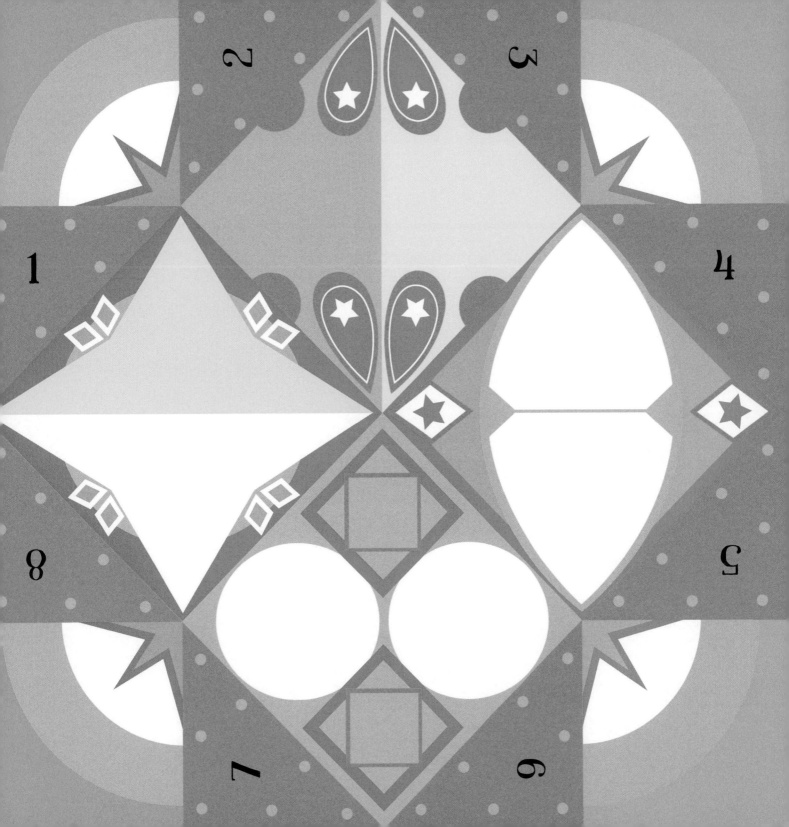

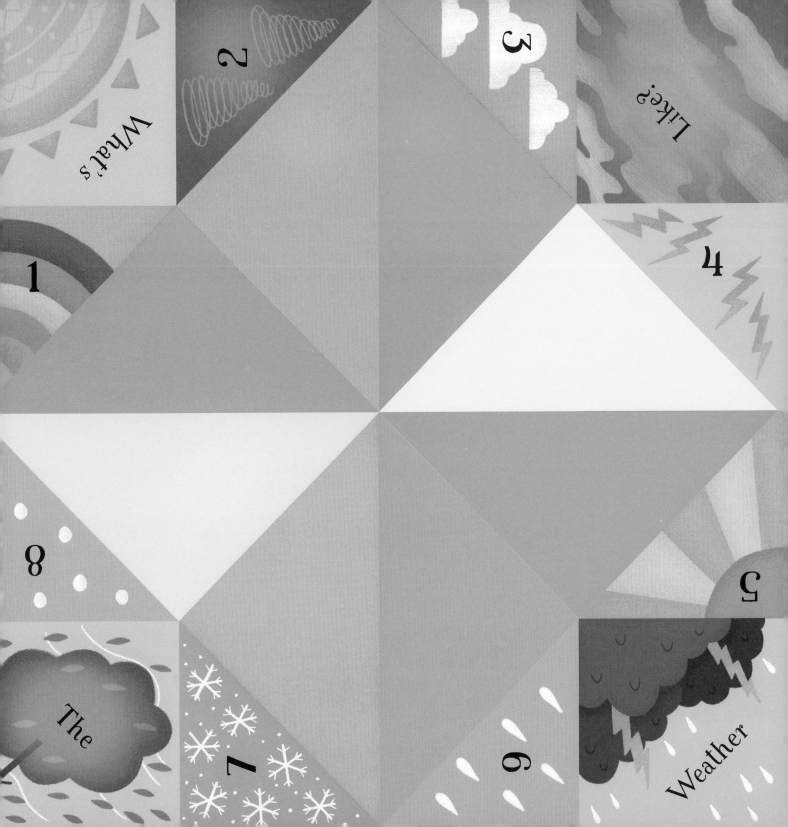

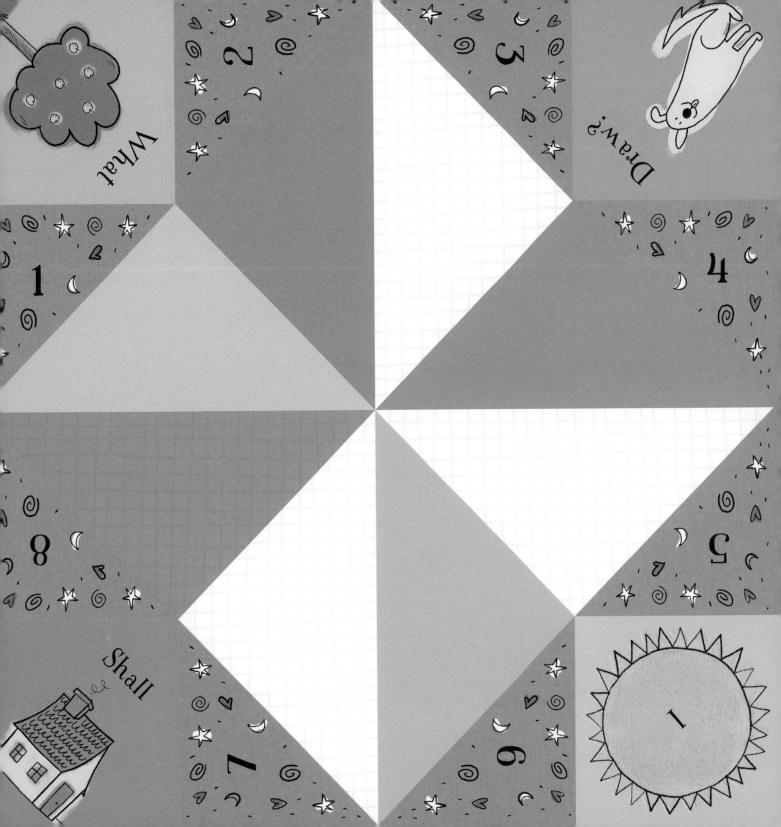

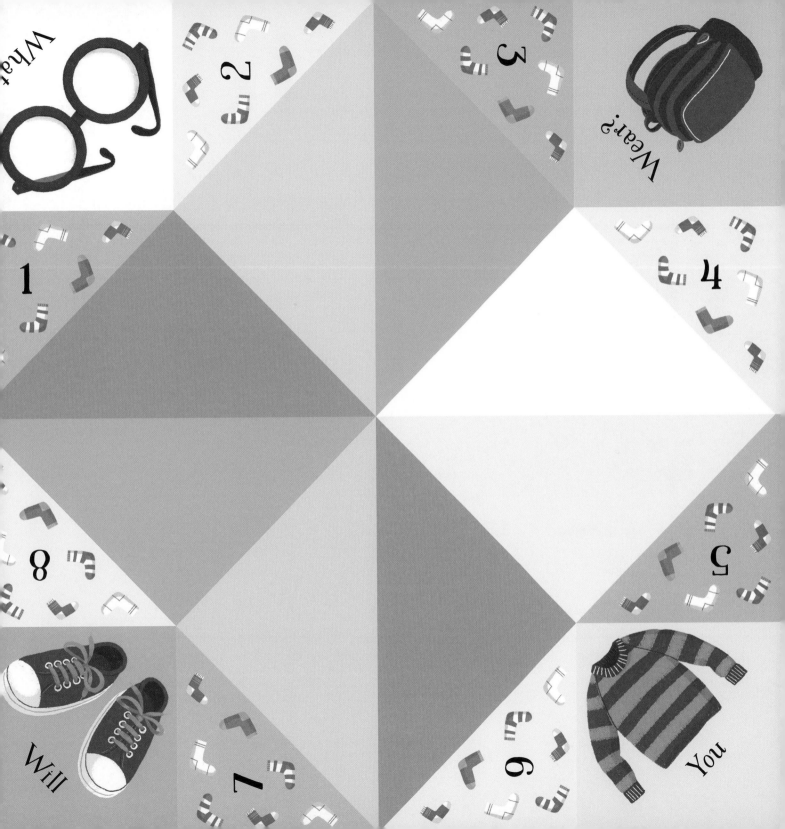

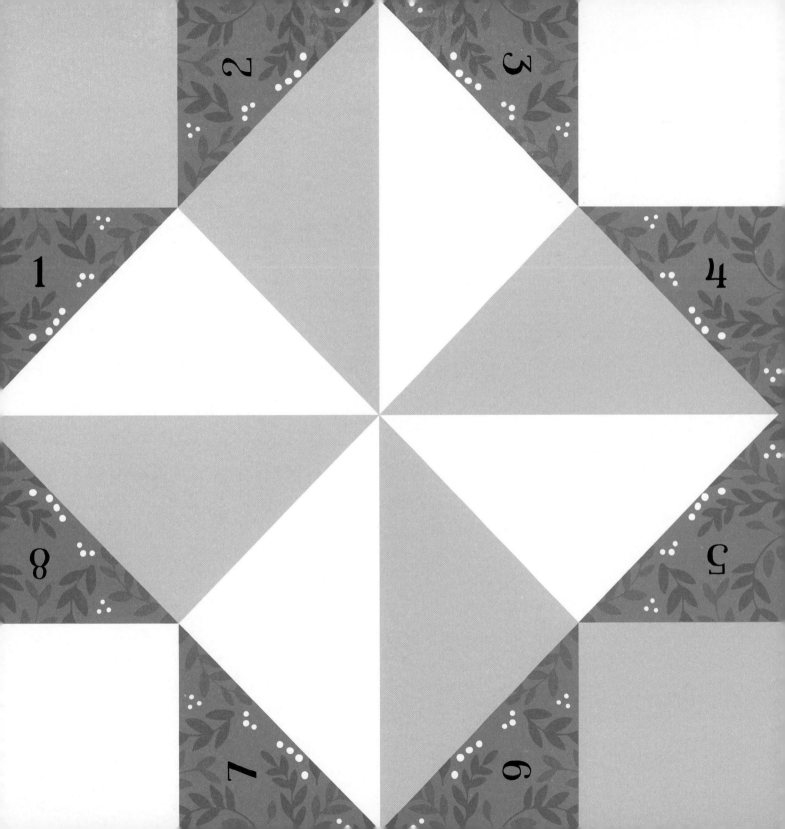

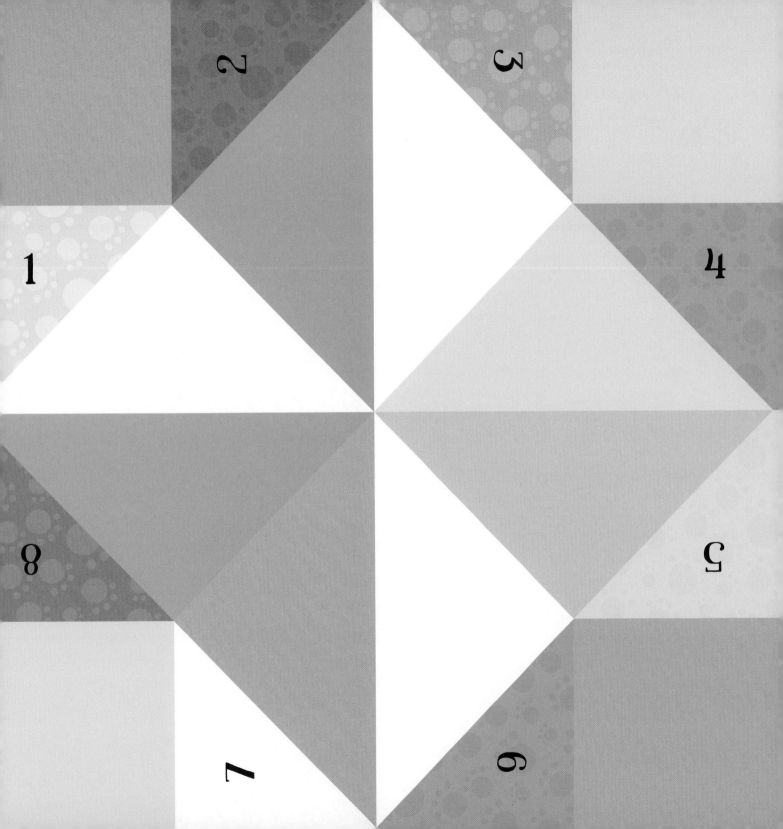

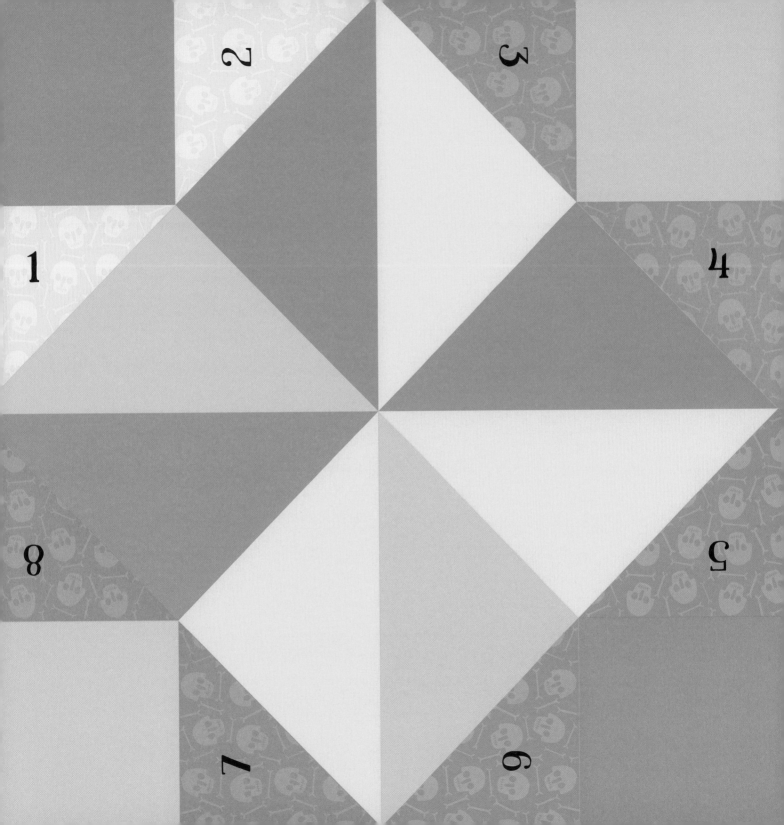

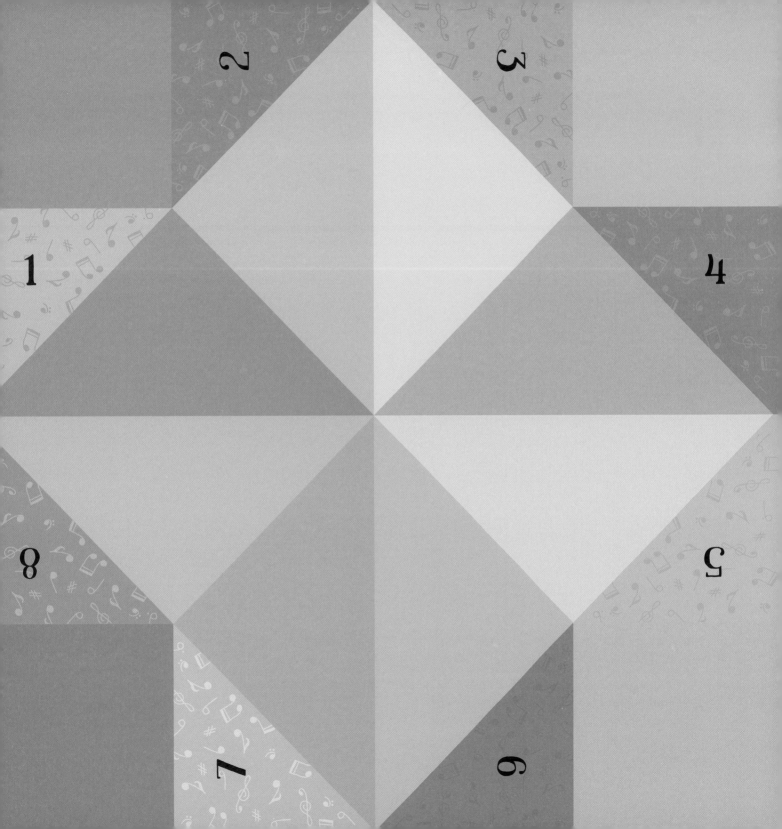

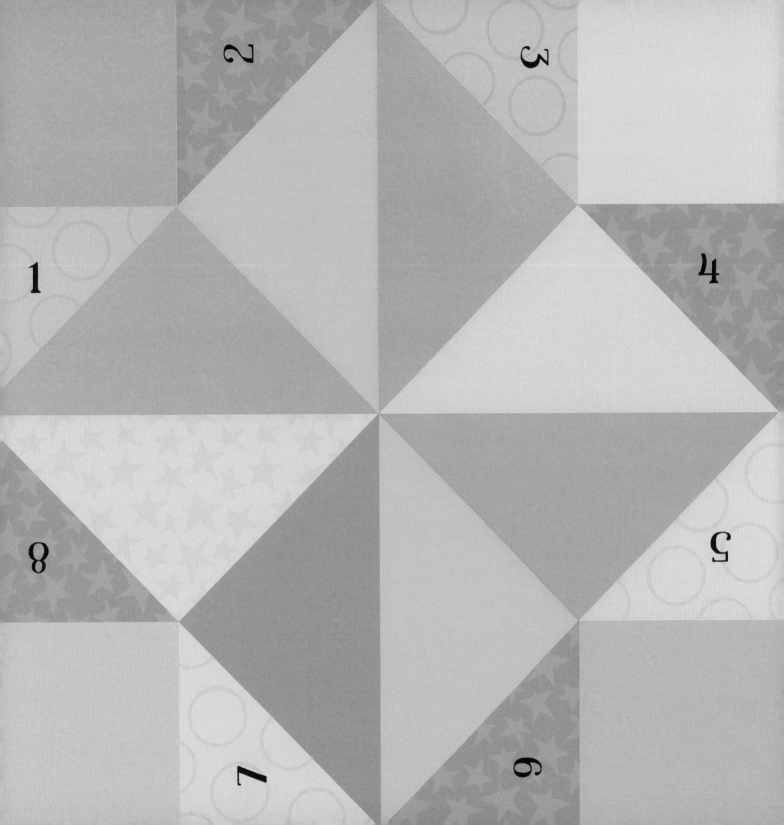

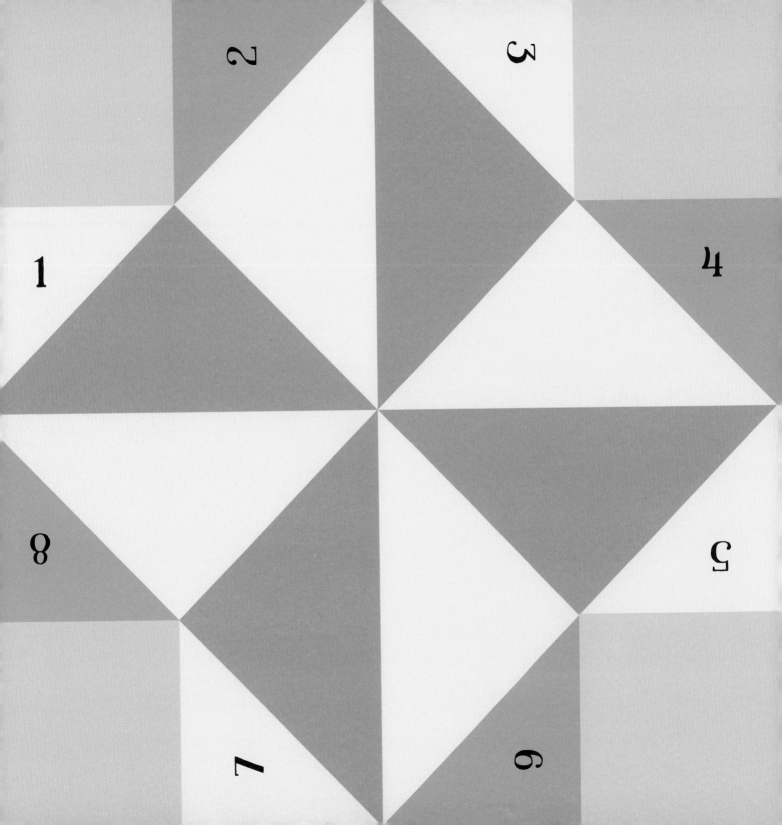

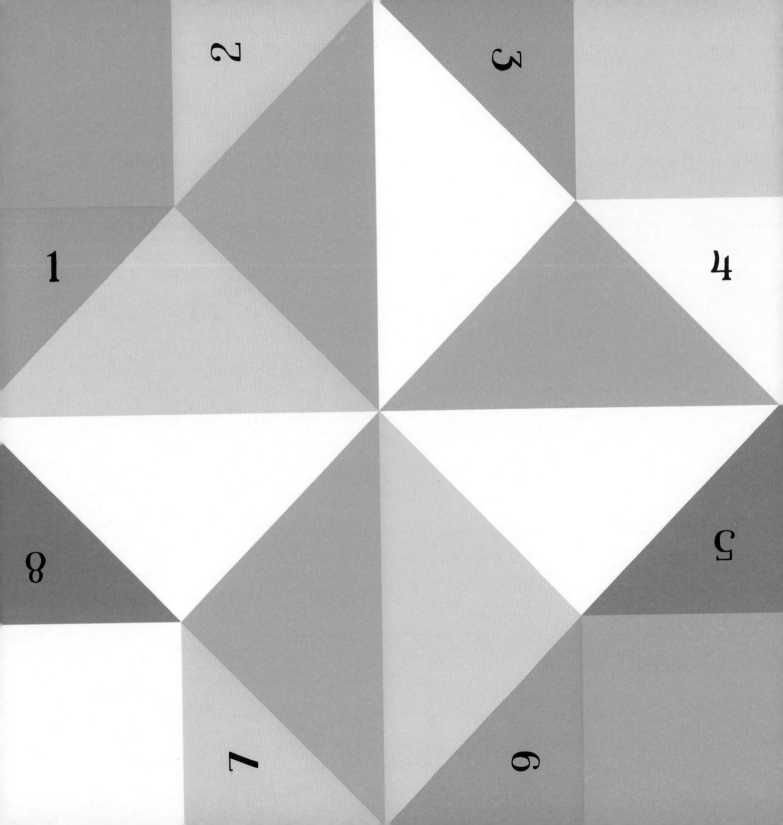

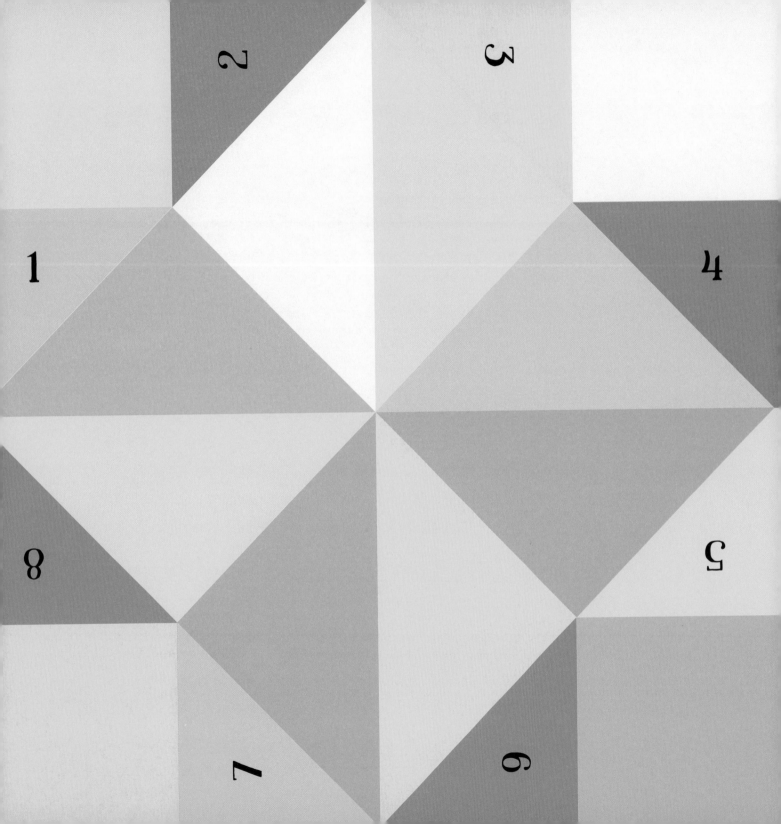